Word List

Here is a list of words that might make it easier to read this book. You'll find them in boldface the first time they appear in the story.

auditorium	au-duh-TOR-ee-um
volunteered	vol-uhn-TEARD
organize	OR-guh-nize
lasso	LAS-o
audience	AU-dee-ens
artistic	ar-TIS-tik
crutch	cruch
comedian	kuh-MEE-dee-uhn
natural	NACH-er-uhl
punch line	PUNCH line
rehearsal	ri-HER-sul
microphone	MY-kruh-fone
confident	KON-fuh-dent
intermission	in-ter-MISH-uhn
announce	uh-NOUNS

Barbie™

The Show Must Go On

©1998 Mattel, Inc. Barbie and associated trademarks are owned and used under license from Mattel, Inc. All Rights Reserved. Published by Grolier Enterprises Inc. Story by Rita Balducci. Photo crew: Scott Fujikawa, Mary Reveles, James LaBianca, Peer Johnson, and Judy Tsuno. Produced by Bumpy Slide Books.
Printed in the United States of America
ISBN: 0-7172-8800-5

Grolier Books

Chapter One

The **auditorium** at Stacie's school was noisy! A talent show was going to be held in three weeks. Everyone was very busy getting ready. Barbie walked in and headed toward the stage. Barbie wasn't just in the show; she had also **volunteered** to **organize** the whole event. All the money made from selling the tickets was going to be used to buy new computers for the school. Barbie couldn't think of a better reason to help.

She went to the old piano and sat down. "Yikes!" she exclaimed when she started playing. The piano was really out of tune.

Barbie played anyway. Soon Stacie came up behind her.

"C'mon, Sis," Stacie said with a grin. "No one wants to hear that stuffy song!" She sat down beside Barbie and began to play the tune "Chopsticks."

Barbie laughed and started to play the song with her sister. The two finished to a round of applause from the tired stage crew. Barbie and Stacie stood up and took a bow.

"You should hear us when the piano is in tune!" exclaimed Barbie.

Suddenly they heard a loud "YEEEE-HA!" A **lasso** swung across the stage and wrapped around Stacie's waist. Barbie looked up and saw Ken dressed in a vest and cowboy hat.

"Howdy-do, little ladies?" he asked.

"Well, I'm a little tied up right now," Stacie answered.

Barbie and Ken laughed.

Stacie stepped out of the lasso. "Mind if I give it a try?" she asked.

"Sure, partner!" Ken replied.

Stacie picked up the rope and began to swing it in circles over her head.

Barbie watched proudly as Stacie twirled the rope as if she had always been a cowgirl. Then she lassoed the hat right off Ken's head!

"Easy, there," Ken said, taking a step back. "You city slickers should leave that sort of thing to a real cowboy!"

Barbie laughed. "Looks like you've met your match, partner," she told Ken.

"Yessiree!" Ken agreed. "That little gal's got a talent for ropin'."

"Thanks!" said Stacie.

"You know," said Ken, "she'd be a perfect addition to the show."

"Oh, no!" Stacie said. She handed the

rope back to Ken. "Not me!"

"Why not?" Barbie asked. "You'd be wonderful. And I sure could use another act to round out the program."

"I don't think I'd like getting up in front of all those people," said Stacie. "Besides, I don't know why you need me. You have lots of exciting acts already."

Stacie looked around the auditorium. All the students were practicing their acts for the talent show. Whitney was singing a song over in one corner. In another corner, Kevin was juggling some plastic bowling pins. Mike, who was going to do a magic act, was trying to get a rabbit into a top hat. Janet was twirling around the stage doing her ballet routine.

"The more the merrier," Barbie told her. "Besides, you'd be helping the school."

"I know," said Stacie.

"Also, the best acts will win a special

prize," added Barbie.

Stacie sighed. She didn't want to let her sister down. "I want to help you, Barbie," she said. "But I'm not sure I'm brave enough to perform in front of a crowd. What if everyone laughs at me?"

Barbie thought for a moment. "What if you *wanted* people to laugh at you?" she asked.

"What do you mean?" wondered Stacie.

"You're so funny!" answered Barbie. "Why not tell jokes? You'd be a hit for sure!"

"Barbie's right," Ken added. "You would be great. I bet the **audience** would love you!"

A grin began to form on Stacie's face. "Do you really think I could do it?" she asked.

"Of course!" said Barbie.

Stacie hugged her sister. "Oh, Barbie! You're so smart!" she said. "At least if people laughed at me, I'd know they liked my act!"

Barbie clapped her hands together. "I can

count on you then?" she asked.

"You bet!" Stacie said. "Count me in!"

Barbie smiled. The show was complete at last!

Chapter Two

Every day Barbie got busier. Organizing a talent show took a lot of work. There was so much to do before the big night. There were tickets and posters and flyers to make. Props had to be built and costumes needed to be sewn. There were sets to put together and paint. It was a big job, but Barbie loved a challenge. Most of all, she loved a good cause.

This afternoon Barbie was helping with the scenery. She was working on a wooden tree. After hanging some paper leaves on it, she stepped back to admire her work.

"Wow, it's really coming together," Barbie thought.

When the tree was finished, Barbie decided to check on Stacie. She found her little sister and her friends standing at a big table. Brightly colored paints and large pieces of poster board were spread all around them. It was their job to make the posters for the talent show.

"Hi, Stacie! How are those signs coming along?" Barbie asked.

"Great!" Stacie said.

"I love all the bright colors," said Barbie. "That will surely get everyone's attention."

"That's the idea!" said Whitney.

Stacie proudly lifted a poster for Barbie to see. "What do you think?" she asked.

The paint was still wet, and the colors began to run down the poster.

"Um, Stacie, maybe you should put that down," Barbie suggested.

Stacie looked down at the poster. "Oops!" she cried. "Should I paint it over?"

Barbie took a good look at the poster. "I think it looks even better!" she said. "It looks more **artistic**!"

"You're right," Stacie agreed. "Maybe we'll make each of the posters look different."

"Good idea!" Barbie said. "But be careful. It looks as if you're painting yourself along with the signs!"

Stacie quickly covered a spot of paint on her skirt with her hand. "Abra-ca-dabra! The paint spot is gone!" Stacie said. "Hey, Sis, maybe I should do a magic act instead of a comedy routine!"

"Very funny!" said Barbie.

"Thank you very much," joked Stacie.

"Now don't forget," said Barbie, "when the posters are dry, you will tape them up around the school, right?"

"No problem!" replied Stacie with a smile.

"We'd be glad to," added Janet.

"Thanks!" said Barbie. "You're all doing a great job!"

Meanwhile, Ken and Christie were backstage. They were unpacking boxes filled with flyers that told the time and date of the show. The flyers would be sent out to everyone in town. Barbie wanted as many people to come as possible. The more people came, the more money the school would raise.

"Uh-oh!" Christie said. She looked into the box of flyers and frowned.

"What's wrong?" asked Ken. He glanced inside the box. "Barbie?"

Barbie walked over to them. "What's up?" she said.

"I didn't know we were having bugs in the show!" said Ken.

"Bugs?" answered Barbie. "What do

you mean?"

Ken grinned and handed Barbie one of the flyers.

ANT TALENT SHOW! it read across the top.

"Oh, no!" Barbie cried. "That's supposed to say GIANT TALENT SHOW!"

"The printer didn't type in the GI at the beginning," Christie said.

Stacie came over and looked at the flyer. "I know," she declared with a playful grin, "let's get a bunch of ants from the garden and dress them up in teeny-tiny costumes."

"They might be kind of hard for the audience to see, though," Ken joked.

"This is serious, you two," said Barbie. But she did find herself giggling. "How long do you think it would take us to write in the missing letters by hand?"

Before anyone could answer, they heard

a loud *thump*. A **crutch** came skidding across the floor and landed at Stacie's feet. A short distance behind it stood Todd, the best soccer player in the whole school. His left leg was in a cast.

"Oops! Sorry!" he laughed. He was trying to balance himself on his other crutch.

"Oh, my goodness! Let me help you!" Barbie cried, jumping up to take his arm.

"I'll help, too!" said Stacie.

Barbie and Stacie helped Todd sit down on a chair beside them.

"I heard you needed help with your cast," Todd said with a twinkle in his eye. "Care to take mine?"

Stacie broke into a giggle.

"Well," Barbie said with a smile, "I'd love to increase our cast of helpers! Are you volunteering?"

"When do I start?" he asked.

"How about right now?" said Barbie.

"No problem!" Todd replied. "What do you want me to do first?"

"How about doing something where you can sit down?" suggested Barbie.

"That's not a bad idea," said Todd.

"Well, it just so happens that we have some flyers that need some quick fixing," Barbie told him.

"Sounds great," said Todd. "I'm happy to help."

Barbie put Todd to work fixing the flyers. He was a fast worker. But later, as he watched his classmates practicing all around him, Todd seemed unusually quiet. Barbie walked over to him.

"Are you okay?" she asked.

Todd tried to sound cheerful. "Oh, sure," he said. "I just wish that I could do more than work on the flyers. I'd like to be *in* the show, too! All the kids look like they're having so

much fun. The problem is, I can't do much on these crutches."

Just then Janet spun past on her toes.

"I certainly can't dance!" Todd declared.

Barbie laughed. "Well, at least you still have your sense of humor!"

Suddenly Todd smiled. "I know what I can do!" he cried.

"What?" asked Barbie.

"I can tell jokes for the show!" said Todd. "I've read so many joke books since I broke my leg. I know them all by heart! What do you think?"

Barbie thought, "Uh-oh! How do I tell Todd that Stacie is already doing a comedy act?" But she knew telling jokes would make Todd happy, too.

"I think you'd make a wonderful **comedian**!" Barbie said.

On the other side of the stage, she saw Stacie

studying her own book of jokes. Barbie wondered how to break the news to Stacie. Would she be upset that Todd was telling jokes in the show, too?

Chapter Three

"Well, honesty is the best policy," Barbie decided.

She took a deep breath and walked up to her sister. "Hey, Stacie, guess what?" Barbie began.

"What?" replied Stacie.

"Todd wants to tell jokes at the talent show, too!" said Barbie. "Isn't that great? After all, there's safety in numbers!"

"Todd?" Stacie said. "Todd the soccer star? Todd the class president? Todd the most popular kid in the whole school? I can't possibly seem funny next to him."

Barbie shook her head. "Don't be silly," she said. "You're just as popular!"

"It's not the same," Stacie said, folding her arms. "Besides, telling jokes was going to be *my* act."

"Come on, Stacie," said Barbie. "There's room enough for two comedians in the show."

But Stacie wouldn't listen. "You don't understand," she said to Barbie.

Barbie put her hand on Stacie's shoulder. "What's the matter?" she asked.

"I can't compete against Todd!" Stacie cried. "No one is going to laugh at my jokes!"

"Sure they will," said Barbie.

"No they won't," cried Stacie. "I can't go onstage now!"

"Stacie," Barbie said gently, "you're taking this much too seriously. You're just as talented as Todd."

"That doesn't matter," Stacie cried.

"You can do it, Stacie," said Barbie. "I promise I'll help you all I can, okay? Don't worry."

Stacie sighed. She knew Barbie was counting on her. But the idea of going up against Todd in the talent show made her stomach hurt. What if the audience didn't think that she was funny? Still, she had given Barbie her word.

"All right," Stacie said at last.

"Great!" Barbie said, giving her sister a hug. "Come on, let's go over some of your jokes."

"Okay," Stacie said with a sigh. She tried not to worry, but she couldn't complete a single joke.

"Geez," said Stacie, "I can't even be funny in front of you. How can I do it in front of a room full of people?"

"I know you can!" Barbie told her. "You're a **natural**!"

But Stacie shrugged. "Maybe later, Barbie," she said. "I just can't think about it right now."

Barbie watched as her sister walked away, leaving her joke book on the floor. She sighed and reached down to pick it up.

Just then, Ken joined Barbie.

"Is something wrong with Stacie?" he asked.

Barbie quickly explained how both Stacie and Todd would be telling jokes in the show. "When I told Stacie, she got very upset," said Barbie. "She feels like she has competition now."

"But Stacie's very funny!" said Ken.

"I know," Barbie agreed. "But maybe letting both of them do comedy acts wasn't such a good idea."

"Barbie, you did what you thought was right," Ken told her. "Don't worry, Stacie will bounce back."

"I hope you're right," said Barbie with a sigh.

Chapter Four

But as the day of the show got closer, Stacie still had a case of stage fright.

"Be funny! Be funny!" she told her reflection in the mirror one Sunday morning.

Her tabby cat stared at her as Stacie began to pace.

"Okay, what do you think of this one?" Stacie asked the cat, bouncing down on the bed beside her. "Tell me if you've heard it before."

The cat yawned and blinked sleepily at Stacie.

"Some audience you are," Stacie said.

Barbie appeared in the doorway. She came in and sat down. "Stacie," she began, "I know you're worried about going onstage. But just remember to relax and let your natural sense of humor guide you. I know you're going to steal the show!"

Stacie frowned. "I'm trying, Barbie, really I am. But just when I think I have a great **punch line**, I remember that Todd is going to tell jokes, too. Then I can't concentrate."

"All you need to do is stop comparing yourself to Todd," Barbie suggested. "You'll each be funny *in your own way*."

"You really think so?" Stacie asked.

"You bet I do!" Barbie replied.

Stacie took a deep breath. "I hope you're right!" she said.

"Well," said Barbie, "there's only one way to find out. Now, why don't you get back to practicing!"

"Are you saying I should hit the books?" Stacie asked. She gave her joke book a slap.

Barbie laughed. "I'm saying that the talent show is less than a week away. And I still haven't heard your routine," she said, folding her arms. "So, as the person in charge of the talent show, and as your sister, I'm asking to hear it. *Please!*"

"Okay, here goes," Stacie said as she took a deep breath. "I flew in from Chicago this morning, and boy, are my arms tired!"

Barbie laughed out loud. "See!" she said. "I knew you had it in you!"

For the rest of the morning, Barbie coached her sister. She helped Stacie remember her punch lines. Barbie laughed loudly at each joke. By the time they were finished, Stacie was feeling much better.

"See what a little practicing can do?" said Barbie.

"Well," said Stacie, "a good audience sure does help!"

Barbie smiled. She was glad to see her sister excited about the talent show again.

Chapter Five

On Monday morning, Stacie had her first challenge. As she and Whitney boarded the school bus, they heard laughter coming from the back. There was Todd, making everyone laugh with jokes from his routine.

Stacie took a deep breath. "I'm not going to let this bother me," she told herself. "As Barbie said, we'll each be funny in our own way."

"Stacie, you're talking to yourself again!" whispered Whitney. They sat down near the front of the bus.

"Oops!" said Stacie. "Don't mind me. I was just thinking about the talent show this weekend."

Whitney nodded. "I know how you feel," she told Stacie. "I keep worrying someone is going to laugh in the middle of my song."

"I've got just the opposite problem," Stacie replied. "I'm afraid that *no one* will laugh during my act!"

"I keep telling myself to relax," Whitney said. "It's supposed to be fun, after all."

"You're right," Stacie agreed.

Another burst of laughter came from the back of the bus.

"Todd really has them rolling in their seats!" noticed Whitney.

"I know," said Stacie, looking out the window. She didn't want Whitney to see how upset she was getting.

"It's so great that he's in the show," said

Whitney. "I wouldn't be surprised if he won first prize. I think we're going to have a sellout crowd after all. Wow, think of all the computer equipment we'll be able to buy! Wouldn't that be great?"

Stacie thought for a moment. "It really would," she had to agree. "I guess it's worth a few butterflies in my stomach!"

The bus pulled up in front of the school. Stacie picked up her backpack and followed the crowd inside. Posters for the talent show were everywhere. Stacie and Whitney smiled at each other as they passed many of the posters they had made themselves.

Stacie walked into her classroom and found that all her classmates were talking about the talent show.

"I can't wait for Saturday night!" Mike said excitedly.

"Me either," cried Erin. "It's going to be so

much fun!"

"My grandma and grandpa are coming to see me!" said Abby.

"Guess what?" Sarah said to Janet. "My mom is making me a costume covered with purple beads! What does yours look like?"

"It's black and pink," replied Janet. "And I think I am going to wear a small crown on my head, like a princess."

"Wow!" said Sarah. "That sounds really neat!"

After Stacie took her seat, her teacher came over to her.

"So, Stacie, I hear you also have a wonderful act planned for the talent show," her teacher said.

"Oh, it's nothing special," Stacie answered quickly. "I'm just helping Barbie."

"Well, I can't wait to see all of you perform!" the teacher said brightly.

Inside Stacie was really thinking, "If everyone would just stop talking about the show,

I'd be a lot less nervous!"

She hated to admit it, but she was beginning to have second thoughts again about going onstage.

Chapter Six

Later that week, Barbie stood in the auditorium with Ken. The talent show was the next night. The **rehearsal** was not going well.

"There's so much work still to be done," she said. "I hope we're ready in time!"

"How about letting me help?" Ken offered.

"You're a lifesaver!" Barbie said gratefully. "You can start by finding Fifi."

"Fifi?" Ken asked, raising his eyebrows.

"She's a French poodle," Barbie explained. "Principal Walsh is doing a trained dog act with his two poodles. One of them is loose somewhere in the building."

"So much for that dog being trained!" Ken said. He turned to leave the auditorium. "Here, Fifi!" he called. "Here, Fifi!"

Barbie looked at her clipboard. There were a lot of acts still to get through. She called the next act to come onstage. "Okay, let's hear it for the juggling talents of Kevin the Great!"

Kevin appeared on the stage with three bowling pins. He threw them up in the air and tried to juggle them. *Crash!* Each one fell to the floor.

"Um, Barbie, can I start again?" he asked.

"Of course!" Barbie told him. "That's why we call this a rehearsal. Now's the time to work out any rough spots in your routine."

Kevin began again. This time he did a really good job of juggling the pins.

"Wow! Terrific!" praised Barbie. "You were juggling so fast, those bowling pins were a blur!"

"Thanks!" Kevin said with a big smile.
He headed offstage.

Barbie looked at her list again. "Mike!" she called out. "Are you and your rabbits ready?"

There was no response.

"Mike?" Barbie called again.

But Ken came onstage. "Um, Barbie?" he said.

"Where's Mike?" asked Barbie. "Is he ready to rehearse his act?"

"He's so good, I don't think he needs much rehearsing," said Ken.

"What do you mean?" asked Barbie.

"Well instead of pulling one rabbit out of a hat," explained Ken, "he's come up with six."

"What?" Barbie cried.

"It seems that his rabbit Charlie must be a Charlotte because she just had a bunch of babies backstage!" said Ken.

"Oh, my!" Barbie exclaimed.

"Don't worry, Barbie," Ken called out. "I found Fifi and I'll take care of the extra rabbits. Then I'll help Mike rehearse."

"Thanks," replied Barbie. She was grateful for all of Ken's help.

Ken walked away saying, "Poodles? Rabbits? Is this a talent show or a pet shop?"

Barbie smiled. "Okay, now back to the rehearsal. Whitney, you're next."

Whitney took her place center stage. One of the members of the stage crew placed a **microphone** in front of her.

"Quiet, please, everyone!" Barbie called out.

Whitney stepped up to the microphone and cleared her throat. The music began to play, and she began to sing. Everyone in the auditorium stopped what they were doing to listen.

Suddenly they heard a *thud!* Whitney jumped in fright, nearly knocking over the microphone.

"What happened back there?" asked Barbie.

A fake gingerbread house had fallen at the back of the stage. "That's what I call bringing down the house, Whitney!" Todd joked from offstage. "Bravo!"

Whitney instantly relaxed and even smiled. Some of the other students began clapping, too. The stage crew began to pick up the gingerbread house.

Barbie sighed. "Thank goodness for Todd," she thought. "He makes everything seem brighter."

Just then Stacie entered the auditorium. Barbie could tell from the look on her sister's face that something was wrong.

"Why don't we all take a ten-minute break?" Barbie said to the performers. "Then Whitney can pick up where she left off."

Barbie was worried about her sister. As the performers left the stage, she went up to Stacie.

"What's up?" Barbie asked her.

"Barbie, I can't be in the show," Stacie said

quickly. "I just can't get up in front of all those people by myself."

Stacie looked really worried. Barbie didn't know if she should even try to change her sister's mind. Then they heard a noise behind them. Barbie turned and saw Todd trying to pick up his crutch. Whitney was holding out her arm to him. "Even Todd needs someone to lean on sometimes," Barbie thought. Then she had an idea.

She looked back at Stacie and smiled. "You may not have to do it by yourself," she answered.

"What do you mean?" asked Stacie.

"Come with me," Barbie said as she took Stacie by the hand. She gently pulled her over to where Todd was standing.

"Hi, you guys," said Todd. "Well, if it isn't the girl who caught my flying crutch," he said to Stacie. "But enough about you . . ."

". . . let's talk about me," Stacie finished.

Todd laughed out loud. "Barbie, you never

told me your sister was so funny," he said.

"You never asked!" Barbie joked.

"Have you heard this one?" Stacie asked. She started to tell her favorite joke. Todd already knew it. He laughed even before the punch line.

"You know, what I like best are the old-time routines," Todd told Stacie. "Like the famous baseball one that starts, 'Who's on first?'"

Stacie nodded excitedly. "I love that one, too!" she cried.

"I have an idea!" said Todd. "Let's combine our routines into one act."

"Really?" said Stacie.

"Sure," said Todd. "I'd feel a lot better performing with a partner."

Stacie was surprised. "Don't tell me you're nervous, too," she said. "You're the school's big soccer star. You play in front of a crowd all the time."

"I do feel **confident** playing soccer," said Todd. "But that doesn't mean I feel confident about being onstage."

"In that case," Stacie said, "you've got yourself a partner!"

"Great!" said Todd. "Let's start practicing!"

Chapter Seven

Finally it was the night of the talent show. Barbie's heart was pounding. She wanted everything to go perfectly. After all, everyone had put in so much hard work. She looked around. All the performers were getting ready. The scenery was in place. Students were taking tickets at the door of the auditorium. Parents were arriving with homemade goodies to sell during **intermission**.

Ken came up to Barbie and gave her a kiss on the cheek.

"Have I forgotten anything?" Barbie asked.

"No, I don't think so," he told her, "except your earrings."

Barbie touched her ears. She felt the earrings she had put on earlier. "Oh, Ken! You're such a kidder!" she said playfully.

"I was just trying to get you to relax," Ken said. "I'm going to get ready now. Good luck!"

"You too!" Barbie exclaimed. She looked out at the audience. She couldn't help but feel excited. The people were settling into their seats as the band started to play. The sight of her neighbors and friends coming out to support the school was something special. "This is going to be a smash!" Barbie said to herself happily.

Just then, Stacie arrived, dressed in a man's fancy suit and a polka-dot tie.

"How do I look?" she asked, spinning around for Barbie's approval.

"Funny!" replied her sister.

"Great!" Stacie answered. "I thought if I

looked funny, I'd feel funny!"

"Good thinking!" said Barbie.

Todd showed up a few minutes later. He wore a top hat and a bow tie.

"Is everybody ready?" Barbie called as the different acts lined up. "Everyone, put on a great show and have fun!" She took a deep breath and walked toward the curtain.

"Break a leg!" called Todd to Barbie in a stage whisper. "Want me to show you how?"

Stacie giggled. Barbie smiled at Todd as she walked out onstage.

"Welcome parents, teachers, and students," Barbie began.

Stacie and Todd listened as Barbie introduced the first act.

"Are you nervous?" Stacie whispered to Todd.

Todd shrugged. "Nah. I was, a little, until you became my partner."

Stacie laughed. "If you only knew how close I came to not performing," she said.

"Well," said Todd, "I'm glad you changed your mind!"

"Me, too!" replied Stacie.

Finally the show began. The poodle act was a hit. Whitney sang better than she ever had before. Ken's lassoing was fast and fancy. Janet's ballet routine was wonderful. And Kevin's juggling was great!

"You're next!" Barbie whispered to Stacie and Todd.

When the audience quieted down, Stacie and Todd went onstage.

Barbie watched from the wings as Stacie started the routine. Barbie felt nervous for her little sister. She wanted Stacie to do really well.

Ken joined Barbie. "They're great!" he said.

Barbie relaxed. She could see Ken was right. By now the audience was howling with

laughter. This gave Stacie the confidence she needed. She really began to enjoy herself. She called out her lines loud and clear. Todd was also having a ball. The audience laughed at the funny faces he made. He and Stacie were a great team!

At last their act was over. Stacie and Todd took a little bow as the audience cheered.

"Thanks! You've been great!" Todd shouted to the audience.

He and Stacie bowed again. But when Todd did, he dropped one of his crutches and began to wobble.

"Easy there!" cried Stacie, grabbing her partner. "No falling down on the job!"

"You'd fall too if you didn't have a leg to stand on!" Todd replied, hopping on one foot.

The audience clapped and cheered. They thought it was all part of the act!

Stacie began to hop, too. "Well, folks,"

she said, "the next act is really terrific. I know you're going to enjoy it. So my partner and I had better hop on out of here!" She steadied Todd, grabbed the crutch, and got the two of them off the stage.

"I don't believe you guys!" Barbie said as Stacie and Todd came through the curtain. "How did you think so fast on your feet?"

"Don't you mean 'off our feet'?" Todd asked with a laugh.

"It was easy!" Stacie said. "We were having so much fun, we didn't want to stop!"

By now the other performers had crowded around them. "Wow! Great job!" they said.

"Thanks, everyone!" said Stacie.

Barbie hugged her sister. "You were terrific," she told Stacie.

"I never could have done it without your help," Stacie said as she hugged Barbie. "Thanks for everything."

"You're welcome," said Barbie. "You and Todd make a great team."

When all the acts were finished, it was time for the prizes.

Principal Walsh came onstage while Barbie played the school's theme song on the piano. She had to try very hard not to wince at the sour notes. The principal asked for one last round of applause for all of the performers. The audience clapped.

Then the principal tapped the microphone, and everyone quieted down. "Good news," he said. "We have reached our goal. Now we will be able to buy all the computers we need!" The audience cheered. "In fact, we even have some money left over, which will be used to . . ." Principal Walsh thought for a moment. "Hmm. Barbie, do you have any ideas on how we might use the extra money?"

"To tune the piano?" Barbie asked

hopefully. Everyone in the audience burst out laughing.

"An excellent idea!" the principal agreed. Then he gave special thanks to Barbie for all her help with the show. Barbie smiled from ear to ear as she came onstage and took a quick bow. Ken followed her onstage and handed her some flowers.

"And now it is time to **announce** the winners," said the principal.

Janet won third place for her ballet dancing. Whitney proudly accepted the award for second prize. And the audience leapt to its feet cheering as Stacie and Todd were announced as the first-prize winners!

Stacie and Todd looked at each other with big smiles. "We did it!" they cried.

"And this year's grand prize is . . . dance lessons!" Principal Walsh said.

The entire auditorium looked at Todd's

cast and began to laugh.

"Great!" Stacie laughed. "Just as long as they're teaching the bunny hop."

The audience laughed even harder.

"Now *that's* what I call funny!" said Barbie.